Running Interference

WRITTEN BY LEIGH OLSEN

Lilly
DIABETES

DISNEY PRESS
New York

Content of book was developed in consultation with Lilly USA, LLC
and is funded by Lilly USA, LLC.

First Edition

10 9 8 7 6 5 4 3 2 1

ISBN 978-1-4231-4706-0
V475-2873-0-12132
PRINTED IN USA
LILLY IS A REGISTERED TRADEMARK OF ELI LILLY AND COMPANY.
ALL RIGHTS RESERVED.

**Looking for tips on family life with type 1 diabetes?
Visit www.family.com/type1**

For more Disney Press fun, visit www.disneybooks.com

Running Interference

Chapter 1

Tim Johnston couldn't stop tossing and turning. No matter how hard he tried, he just couldn't seem to get comfortable. A million thoughts were racing through his mind.

Tim flipped over in bed and looked at his clock. *11:11 p.m.* Ugh. At this rate, he was going to be exhausted by the time he had to get up for school in the morning. It was the night before the first day of eighth grade, and the last thing he wanted was to start things off on the wrong foot. After all, this was *eighth grade*. Tim had looked up to the eighth graders since his first day at Haddon Middle School. Cool, calm, and confident, they knew their place as the eldest kids in school. And now, finally, he'd be one of them.

It didn't hurt that Tim was the starting cornerback for the school's football team. He'd worked hard for the position, and he'd earned it. Now that fall had finally arrived, there were games and pep rallies to look forward to—not to mention an entire team of football buddies to hang out with.

But if being an eighth grader and a member of the football team was supposed to make him feel confident about his first day of school, it wasn't working. And he knew why.

Tim had been diagnosed with type 1 diabetes over the summer, and tomorrow would be his first day back at school. Tim had gotten used to taking care of himself over the summer, but managing his diabetes during the school day was going to be a completely different story. He wasn't sure how he'd manage to pay attention in school and take care of his diabetes, too. It was going to be a challenge, and he knew it.

And to make matters worse, Tim had missed preseason training camp because it took place so soon after his diagnosis. That meant he'd be starting practice later than the rest of his team. He'd been exercising on his own, but he hadn't been able to train with his teammates since last season. Luckily, his coach knew Tim was a hard worker, and even though he missed preseason training, he let Tim keep his starting position. After all, he had *earned* the position. But Tim was worried about starting out behind the rest of his teammates.

Tim's friends on the football team already

knew about his diagnosis. They'd had a team meeting last week to go over their practice schedule and Tim had told them about his type 1 diabetes, but Tim had promised himself he wouldn't make a big deal out of it. He wasn't big on being the center of attention, and he wanted to be known for his football skills—not his diabetes.

Tim shook all of these thoughts from his head. He *had* to get to sleep. As he began to count sheep, his mind finally drifted off. . . .

Beep! Beep! Beep!

Tim reluctantly shook himself awake as his alarm clock pulled him out of his dream. It seemed like he had just fallen asleep. How was it already time to get up for school?

Tim dragged himself into the bathroom for a quick shower and then headed downstairs for breakfast. Although Tim saw his dad occasionally, he and his younger sister, Kayla, lived with their mom full-time. His parents had gotten divorced when he was little.

"Morning, Timmy!" Kayla hollered as she raced past him.

Tim's little sister had more energy than anyone he knew. Even her clothes seemed energetic. Today she wore an outfit of such screamingly loud colors, Tim thought his sleepy morning eyes might be blinded by the sight!

Today was Kayla's first day of sixth grade, which meant the two siblings would be at school together for the first time since Tim had been in elementary school. Somehow, Tim had no doubt his adorable little sis would survive the harsh hallways of middle school just fine. Though it didn't hurt, he thought to himself with a smile, that she had a cool eighth-grade brother to look out for her.

"Scrambled eggs?" asked Tim's mom.

"Yes, please," Tim said as his mom put a hearty serving on his plate.

"And here's some fruit salad," she added. "There's whole wheat toast, too."

"Blech," said Kayla. "I *hate* whole wheat. Can't I just have a bowl of Frosted O's, Mom?"

"Frosted O's don't have much nutritional value," Tim's mom said. "You're a growing girl. You need a healthy and well-balanced breakfast. We should all be starting off our day with a nice, healthy meal."

Tim had to pay close attention to what he ate now that he had diabetes. In particular, he had to keep track of the carbohydrates in his food because they affected his blood sugar level the most. His dietitian had also helped him pick out overall healthier foods that she explained were good for everybody.

"You can still eat your Frosted O's sometimes," Tim said to his sister through a mouthful of eggs. "You can do what I do, and have them every now and then as a special treat."

Kayla nodded. "You're right," she said. "Anyway, I know I'll have a better first day of middle school if I eat a good breakfast."

Tim's mom turned to her son. "I've put some glucose tablets and your glucose meter in your backpack. I also spoke with the school nurse, and she knows you will be coming to her office for your insulin at lunch today."

This would be the first time Tim had given himself a shot when he wasn't with his mom, and he was nervous. It made him feel a little better that his mom had spoken with the school nurse, though. He knew she'd be well equipped to help him out.

"And you packed up a bunch of snacks last night, right?" his mom asked.

"Yup!" Tim responded, holding up his

backpack. "Guess I'm all set."

Tim's mom glanced at her watch. "You kids had better get going. The bus will be on the corner any minute now."

Tim and Kayla each gave their mom a hug good-bye. Then the two siblings headed out to the bus stop at the entrance to their cul-de-sac.

Chapter 2

Tim and Kayla watched the big yellow school bus round the corner. When it slowed to a stop, Tim climbed aboard. His best friend, Hank, was in the back, waving to him.

The bus started to move as Tim clambered down the aisle to a back seat. This was one of the perks of being an eighth grader—being able to claim the back of the bus.

"Hey, man," Hank exclaimed, a wide grin

on his kind, round face. "You ready to go back?"

"As ready as I'm going to be," Tim said, smiling. "Hey, can I see your class schedule?"

Tim put their schedules side by side. "Cool," he said. "We've got homeroom together again."

Tim was excited. He and Hank had been best friends since the third grade, when Hank had moved to Tim's neighborhood. Hank was on the football team with Tim, too. In fact, they both played cornerback.

"Are you going to football practice tonight?" Hank asked, breaking into Tim's thoughts.

"Yeah," Tim answered. He was nervous just thinking about it.

"Well, it'll be awesome to have you back," Hank said. "Coach Purcell said he's going to take it easy on us, considering it's our first week back to school and all."

Tim breathed a sigh of relief. At least he could ease himself back into the game a little bit.

A few minutes later, the school bus pulled up to Haddon Middle School. Tim and Hank got off the bus, joining the sea of students streaming through the front doors.

As he looked around at the familiar faces, Tim took a deep breath. This was the start of his third year here, yet he couldn't help feeling like eighth grade was going to be completely different from the school years before it.

"Bye, Tim!" Kayla waved as she found a gaggle of girlfriends.

Tim waved to his little sis, and he and Hank made their way to homeroom.

In Mrs. Veela's class, Tim pulled out his schedule again. Homeroom was followed by history, Spanish, math, and then lunch. Tim was anxious about not being able to check his blood sugar level quite as easily as he had been able to at home. He felt fine, but it was driving him nuts that he couldn't privately grab his glucose meter and check to find out for sure that he was okay. He knew that if he really wanted to, he could take a reading at any time, but he really didn't want to draw any extra attention to himself. So he set his mind to focusing on school. But even with all the new classes, teachers, books, and a homework assignment, the morning was crawling by. Tim checked the clock constantly, only to see that it had hardly moved at all. His nervousness built as the lunch hour slowly approached. Was his blood sugar okay?

Finally, in the beginning of math class, Tim made up his mind. He'd go down to the nurse's office and check his blood sugar level.

Taking a deep breath, Tim raised his hand.

"Yes, Tim?" asked his teacher Ms. Duffy.

"May I please be excused?"

Ms. Duffy looked at Tim quizzically for a moment. Tim was worried that she'd forgotten about his diabetes and was going to ask him why he needed to leave class. But, to his relief, a look of recognition finally registered on her face. "Of course," she said. "Just take the hall pass with you."

Tim picked up his backpack and grabbed the large metal colander that served as Ms. Duffy's hall pass. He felt several pairs of eyes on him as he left the classroom. He hoped they weren't wondering too much about where he was going with his backpack in the middle of class.

Tim walked quickly down the hallway, finally reaching the nurse's office.

"Can I help you?" the nurse asked.

"Hi," Tim said shyly. "I'm Tim. I'm . . . diabetic, and I wanted to check my blood sugar level."

"Oh, Tim, of course!" the nurse said, smiling warmly. "You can go ahead and have a seat."

Tim nodded and sat down to check his level. As he suspected, everything was fine. But he felt relieved now that he had checked. He thanked Nurse Swanski and headed back to class, which at this point was about halfway over. *Oh well,* he thought. It was smarter to go to Nurse Swanski's office and make sure his level was okay than to have stayed in class worrying. He was going to have to start getting used to this kind of interruption.

Back in math class, Tim willed himself to ignore the curious looks he was getting from some of the other kids. He settled into his seat and waited for the bell to ring. Finally it was time for lunch. Tim felt a little silly as he made his way back to the nurse's office yet again. This time for his insulin. He'd felt okay about going before, but this time he was nervous. Nurse Swanski seemed really nice, but only his mom and his diabetes team had ever helped him with his insulin before.

"Ah, Tim," Nurse Swanski said. "It's nice to see you again. You ready for your insulin?" she asked.

"Yup," Tim replied.

"All right, well come on back, and we'll get you off to lunch in a jiffy."

Tim followed Nurse Swanski to the small room he'd visited earlier. While the nurse got his insulin, Tim took another reading with his glucose meter. He showed Nurse Swanski the reading. As she checked his insulin dose, she started up a friendly conversation.

"So your mom said you got diagnosed this summer, huh?" she asked.

"Yeah," Tim replied.

"And it's your first day back at school with

diabetes," she said. "That must be kind of tough."

"I guess so," Tim answered. "I try not to make a big deal about it, but it's hard not to think about."

"I understand," said Nurse Swanski. "It's not easy being at school when you're still trying to get used to managing your diabetes. You have to get yourself accustomed to a new schedule, to new eating times, and to dealing with it in front of your friends."

"Exactly," Tim said, nodding.

Nurse Swanski's easy manner made Tim feel less nervous. He quickly gave himself his insulin. He was proud of how good he'd gotten at doing this already.

"Well," Nurse Swanski continued, "there's a student here. He and his parents asked me to give his name to anyone who has been diagnosed with type 1 diabetes and might need a friend who understands. His name is

Roger Jablonski, and he was diagnosed with type 1 diabetes several years ago. He comes in here every day to give himself his insulin. His lunch period is the same as yours. If you ever need someone to talk to about what you're going through, he'd be a great resource for you. Of course, it's totally up to you. If you're not interested, that's fine. Don't worry, I won't tell Roger anything about you."

Tim had had a few classes with Roger. He was an eighth grader, too. Roger was, to put it mildly, a bit of an awkward guy. He was tall and seriously gangly. He was super-smart, but he also had a tendency to talk really, *really* loudly and to spurt out random things from time to time. He was a little bit nerdy, Tim supposed, but maybe the two had more in common than he thought.

"Here," Nurse Swanski said, grabbing a piece of paper and a pen. "Roger gave me his phone number in case anyone was interested in taking him up on his offer. I'll give it to you in case you want it. I think you two might just get along. You both seem like good kids."

She scribbled down Roger's phone number in sprawling purple ink and passed the slip of paper over to Tim.

"Thanks," he mumbled, shoving the paper into his jeans pocket. As he left Nurse Swanski's office, he gave it some thought. Roger seemed like a nice enough guy. Nurse Swanski was right about that. But what would his football friends think of him hanging out with someone like Roger?

Chapter 3

The noisy table in the back of the crowded room was crammed with football players, Hank among them. Tim let out a sigh of relief. After a hectic morning, it would be nice to hang out with his friends for a bit.

"Hey," Tim said casually, sidling up to a seat between Hank and Sam, one of the football team's offensive tackles.

Sam was a huge guy for an eighth grader.

But he was also incredibly quick on his feet, which made him great at his position. He was also one of the most popular guys at school. Sam was always nice to Tim and his other football friends, but he could sometimes be a real pain to the less popular students. Tim didn't like that, but as long as he was being nice to Tim . . .

"Hey, man," said Sam. "It's good to have you back. How come you're late to lunch?"

"I had to go to the nurse's office," Tim said.

"Are you feeling all right?" Hank asked.

"Yeah, just had to get my insulin," Tim said, taking out the contents of his lunch bag. He had a sandwich, an apple, some almonds, a handful of whole wheat crackers, and a sliced-up cucumber. Sure, his lunch was healthy, but it wasn't exactly exciting. He looked wistfully at Sam's pile of nachos, which were slathered with cheese, sour cream, and all the trimmings. "Man, I wish I had your nachos right now," Tim said with a laugh.

"Yeah, what's up with your packed lunch?" Sam asked. "You always buy lunch with us."

"Right now it's easier to pack my own lunch. I need to know what's in the food I'm eating, and I'm still getting the hang of counting my carbs. This way my mom and I can plan my meal together, and I know how much insulin I need to take."

Tim was bummed about staying away from cafeteria foods, but he knew for now it would make the adjustment to handling his diabetes at school easier. He was, he noticed, the only one of his friends who brought lunch. It was just one other thing that, thanks to his diabetes, made him feel different from the rest of them. He couldn't wait until he had the hang of planning his meals so he could start buying food at school again.

"It stinks that you have to bring a bagged lunch," Hank said, pulling Tim out of his thoughts.

"Yeah." Tim hesitated. "I mean, at least my mom makes a mean turkey sandwich," he added with a chuckle, trying to lighten the conversation. He appreciated that his friends were curious about his diabetes, but he didn't want to dwell on the topic.

"How's everyone's first day going?" he asked.

"Can't complain," said Joe, a wide receiver. "But, man, I can't believe Señora Jackson gave us homework already!"

"Tell me about it," said Henry Gellar, the quarterback and team captain. "You're supposed to get books and play the name game on the first day of school. You're not supposed to actually *do* anything."

With a chuckle, Tim nodded his head in agreement. "I know," he said, taking a bite of his turkey sandwich. As he did, he realized his mom had forgotten to pack him a bottle of water.

"I'll be right back," he said, scrounging a few quarters out of his backpack. "I'm gonna go get a drink."

Tim walked out the back door of the cafeteria to the hallway where the vending machines stood. With his diabetes, Tim tried to stick to sugar-free drinks with his lunch. But as he scanned the vending machine, he didn't see any. There was no bottled water, either.

Frustrated, he pocketed his quarters.

Tim sighed, heading back into the cafeteria to get a cup that he could fill up with water from the water fountain. It was bad enough that he had to balance school and his diabetes. But now it seemed like the school was making life *more* difficult for him. How did other kids with diabetes manage? They were probably just as frustrated as he was.

Chapter 4

After school, Tim headed down to the locker room, where he and the rest of his teammates got ready for their first after-school football practice. The guys were hollering and messing around with each other as they suited up, but Tim didn't get any of the inside jokes they were making. He wished he hadn't missed out on preseason training. Now he just felt out of the loop.

Tim went over to the small bag he'd

brought with him containing his glucose monitor, sat down on a bench, and took a reading. He noticed a few of his teammates watching him. He didn't like the attention, but he knew this was an important part of taking care of his diabetes. Tim had done some light exercise over the summer, but he wasn't sure how a strenuous workout would affect his blood sugar. He was glad to see that everything looked fine for him to begin exercising.

"All right, guys," Coach Purcell shouted. "Let's get out on the field and warm up!"

Tim packed up his monitor and headed outside with his friends.

The team jogged a mile to warm up and then Coach Purcell got them started doing sprints.

When it was Tim's turn to run his first sprint, he found that it took all his effort to keep up with the other guys. A half an hour of brutal sprints later, Tim's body ached, and he felt out of breath. He just wasn't at the level of fitness the other boys were.

"Seriously," Tim said to Hank. "Coach Purcell calls this *taking it easy* on us?"

Hank shrugged, wiping the sweat from his brow. "You should have seen some of the practices we went through at preseason training," he said. "They were ridiculous. The number of miles we ran, you'd think we were cross-country runners, not football players."

Tim didn't say anything in response. At least if he had been at those summer practices, he wouldn't feel so out of shape now. He had to admit that no one else on the team seemed to be struggling to keep up as much as he was. But then, they'd had more time to get in shape.

When the boys had caught their breath, Coach Purcell had the team do some simple throwing and catching exercises. Tim paired up with Hank. At first everything seemed fine. Then, suddenly, he started to feel a bit woozy. He clutched his head, which felt very heavy.

"You okay?" said Hank. "Tim?"

Tim nodded and dragged himself back over to his bag.

His teammates stopped what they were doing and began to gather around him.

"What's going on?" he heard someone ask.

"I don't know. Maybe he's sick," another voice responded.

Out of the corner of his eye, Tim saw Coach Purcell jog over. "It's all right, guys," the coach said. "Back to your exercises."

The crowd dispersed. "You're having a low, Tim, is that right?" Coach Purcell asked.

Tim nodded. He realized he had forgotten to have a snack to keep up his blood sugar.

"I need to take some glucose tablets," he told the coach.

"All right," Coach Purcell said. "You just let me know if you need anything."

Tim shakily opened his bag and grabbed a few glucose tablets, popping them in his mouth. Hank sat down beside him, talking nonchalantly, trying to reassure Tim as he waited for his blood sugar to come back up.

After about fifteen minutes, Tim began to feel normal again. He turned to Coach Purcell, who was still standing nearby, a concerned look on his face. "I'm doing much better, Coach," Tim told him.

"Good, I'm happy to hear it," Coach Purcell said. "Take a little break, all right? No need to rush getting back to work."

Tim nodded. "Okay," he said.

Now that he was feeling better, Tim noticed that his teammates kept stealing glances at him. They were trying to be subtle, but

Tim was sure they probably thought he was totally weird. Or that he was so out of shape, he couldn't even manage a measly after-school practice. He wondered how often this kind of thing was going to happen to him. The thought of a repeat occurrence just made him feel worse.

When practice was over, Tim showered and changed. Then he grabbed his things and walked out of the locker room to meet his mom. On his way to the car, Tim walked past Sam, Henry, Hank, and Joe, who were talking quietly outside the school entrance. When they spotted Tim, they suddenly went quiet. The hairs on the back of Tim's neck prickled. Had they just been talking about him?

"Hey, man," said Henry. "You doing better now?"

"Yeah," said Joe. "Hank said your diabetes was acting up or something."

"I had low blood sugar, that's all," said Tim. "I'm fine now."

"All right, that's good," said Hank.

Tim felt awkward. He just wanted to go home. "I gotta go," Tim said hurriedly. "My mom's waiting. I'll see you guys tomorrow."

After he climbed into the passenger seat of his mom's car, Tim pulled Roger's phone number out of his pocket and looked at it. Maybe Nurse Swanski had a point. It might make him feel a whole lot better to talk to someone else who was going through what he was.

Chapter 5

By the time Tim got home, he was exhausted. He ate dinner with his family and went up to his room. He pulled out the slip of paper Nurse Swanski had given him. He felt a little weird calling someone who was almost a complete stranger. But he'd had such a rough day. Maybe talking to someone who could relate would help after all.

Finally, he picked up the phone and dialed Roger's phone number.

Someone answered on the first ring. "Hello?" said the urgent voice on the other end.

"Um, hi," Tim said. "Is Roger there?"

"Speaking!" exclaimed the voice.

"Hi, Roger, my name's Tim Johnston. I'm not sure if you remember me. We've had a couple of classes together."

"Oh, hey, Tim!" said Roger, his voice filled with surprise. "Of course I know who you are."

"Cool," Tim said. "Well, anyway, Nurse Swanski, the school nurse, gave me your name."

"Ahh, the Swansk!" Roger exclaimed. "She's a great old gal. Nice lady."

Tim didn't know if he'd ever spoken to someone so enthusiastic in all his life. Every word Roger spoke was loud and excited-sounding. He was definitely a friendly guy; there was no doubt about that.

"Uh, yeah," Tim said. "The thing is, I got diagnosed with diabetes this summer, and she said you went through the same thing a few years ago."

"Yeah," Roger said. "I've had diabetes for six years now. Feels like forever! Anywho, I'm glad the Swansk gave you my info. I know it's not easy, what you're going through, that's for sure! But no need to fear, Roger Jablonski is here!"

Tim was a little taken aback by Roger's excitement. He began to wonder if it had been a good idea to call him after all.

"Well, great," Tim said. "I guess I was just wondering if . . . you had any tips or anything, you know, for, like . . ." Tim trailed off. He wasn't really sure how to ask a near stranger for help like this.

Roger, sensing Tim's hesitancy, piped in. "I understand," he said. "Sometimes it just helps to know you're not the only person who has gone through what you are going through. When I was diagnosed, I remember feeling so lost. And I remember feeling like I was the only person who was going through it, like I didn't have anyone to talk to."

It was as if Roger were reading Tim's mind. Tim was thankful he didn't have to spell it out for him. He wasn't always so good at that touchy-feely stuff.

"So why don't we just get together sometime, you know?" Roger continued. "I can tell you more about my story with diabetes, and you can tell me yours."

"Okay," Tim said. "That sounds like a good plan." Meeting in person would probably feel less strange than talking on the phone.

"How about we go to the Koffee Klatch for some hot cocoa? They're the only place in town that has sugar free," Roger exclaimed. "Maybe Wednesday?"

Tim hesitated. "I've got football practice after school that day," he said.

"That's all right, I've got chess club after school on Wednesday," said Roger. "We'll meet at the Koffee Klatch afterward."

"Great," Tim said. "I'll see you then."

"Adios!" said Roger, hanging up the phone.

Tim already felt a little better. Yes, Roger was kind of unusual, to say the least. But he was extremely nice to go out of his way to help Tim like this. Maybe, Tim hoped, Roger wasn't actually as strange as he seemed.

Chapter 6

At Wednesday's football practice, Coach Purcell split up the team by position and had the players run drills. Since Tim and Hank were both cornerbacks, Coach had them spend the entire practice doing agility and tackling drills. At the moment, they were backpedaling up and down the field.

"I can't believe our first game is a week from Friday," Tim said, panting as he struggled to keep up with his best friend. The

Haddon Middle School Hornets were going to be playing the Grier City Greyhounds. The two were the biggest rivals in the league, and this was hands down the biggest game of the regular season. There would be a pep rally at Haddon during the school day, and there was sure to be a big crowd at the game.

Tim was excited, but he was nervous, too. He hoped he'd feel more prepared in a week, because right now, even though he was doing his best to keep up with the rest of the team, he still felt behind.

It didn't help that Tim had to take breaks to check his blood sugar. After his low at practice the other day, he was even more aware of the guys looking at him. He tried to act like it was no big deal, but it was tiresome, Tim had discovered, pretending he wasn't preoccupied with his diabetes. In fact, he was thinking about it all the time.

Suddenly, Coach Purcell blew his whistle.

"Ten-minute break!" he called. "Get some water and stretch out, everyone."

"Hey, man," said Sam, catching up with Tim and Hank. Sam was sweating profusely. "Geez, am I beat. I've been hitting the sled all practice," he added, describing the padded apparatus the offensive linemen used to practice blocking.

Hands on hips as he caught his breath, Tim gave a weak smile to Sam.

"Looks like I'm not the only one who's struggling, huh?" said Sam with a chuckle.

Tim turned beet red and looked down at the ground. The last thing he wanted was for his teammates to notice that he was lagging behind.

"Hey, give the guy a break, Sam," said Hank, giving Sam a knowing look.

"Sorry, dude," said Sam loudly. "But it looks like you might have to pick up the pace real fast."

As if Tim didn't already know that.

Hank caught Sam's eye again. "What?" Sam asked defensively. "I'm only joking. You know that, right, Tim?"

"Sure," Tim said, giving Sam a small smile. Sam was being kind of a jerk, but Tim figured he was right. Missing preseason practice had set him back, and he'd have to kick it up a notch in order to get where he needed to be.

As if to break the tension, Coach Purcell called for a brief scrimmage before the end of practice. The offense and defense lined up on either side of the fifty-yard line. The center hiked the ball to Henry. Tim found the guy he was supposed to cover—Joe, the wide receiver. But before he could catch up to him, Henry threw the ball. It arced right over Tim's head and directly into Joe's hands.

"Where were you, man?" said Sam, looking exasperated. "Joe was wide open."

Tim sighed. He just couldn't get his head in the game. He was too distracted by his worries over falling behind. The team lined up again and again, but Tim's confidence was shot, and he failed to stop the offense from scoring twice more.

As the team hit the locker rooms after practice, Tim found himself walking behind the rest of the team.

"You all right, man?" asked Henry. "You seem a little down."

"Yeah," said Tim, forcing a smile onto his face. "Just a tough practice."

"It's all right," said Henry with a smile. "I get that. We all know what you've been going through, and no one's holding it against you that this is your second practice back. We're just glad to have you with us again."

"Thanks," Tim said.

Tim joined up with Hank and Sam and a few other guys on their way out of the locker room. At the front entrance to the school, he saw a line of cars: parents waiting to take their sons home.

"Well, I'll see you guys tomorrow," Tim said as he began to wander down the sidewalk.

"Don't you want a ride home?" Hank asked him.

"Yeah, where are you off to?" asked Sam.

Tim didn't know what to tell them. For some reason he was embarrassed that he was going to meet Roger for hot chocolate.

"Oh, uh . . . just going to study," he said. "You know, over at the Koffee Klatch," he added.

"On the first week of school?" asked Joe.

"Nerd!" said Sam jokingly.

Tim chuckled. "Yeah, yeah," he said. "We'll see who's laughing when I'm the only one of us who passes Señora Jackson's class!"

His friends laughed.

"See ya," said Hank.

Tim walked off down the sidewalk. The Koffee Klatch was just across the street from the school parking lot. He felt a little guilty that he didn't want his friends to know he was hanging out with Roger. It wasn't like Roger was a total weirdo or anything. But like his diabetes, Tim worried that his friends just wouldn't understand.

Chapter 7

"Tim-bo! Over here!" Tim heard a voice call.

He looked up to see Roger waving exuberantly from a booth toward the back of the Koffee Klatch. At the moment, the place was pretty quiet, with a few students studying. Tim didn't think there was any need to shout. And what was with this "Tim-bo" business? Tim took a deep breath and walked over to Roger.

"You want to get a drink?" Roger asked Tim. Roger already had a steaming mug of hot chocolate in front of him.

Tim smiled and set down his bag. "You bet. I'll be right back," he said. The barista handed Tim his small hot chocolate, and he rejoined Roger at the table.

The two started out by talking about the first week of school. Roger was eager to hear Tim talk about football.

"I've always been a big football fan," Roger said. "I've just never been really athletic."

"I've always been a big fan, too," said Tim. "And I love playing, though every time I'm out on the field lately, it seems like my mind is somewhere else. I think I just need to get back in the swing of things," Tim added. At least, he hoped that was the case.

Roger told Tim all about what he had been up to recently: namely, preparing for a big chess tournament on Saturday. He got all worked up telling Tim a funny chess story.

"And then he goes, 'Here's *rooking* at you, kid!'" Roger let out a whoop of laughter. "Isn't that hilarious?"

Tim didn't really get the chess joke, but he let out a small laugh, anyway. When he glanced to his side, he noticed a kid who was studying give him and Roger a dirty look. Tim shrugged it off. Nothing wrong with being excited, he told himself.

"So, you got diagnosed this summer, huh?" Roger asked. "How are you handling it?"

"Okay, I guess," Tim said. "There are a few things I'm struggling with, though, like watching everything I eat and counting carbs."

"Tell me about it," said Roger. "That stuff took me forever to figure out."

"Really?" said Tim.

"Yeah," said Roger. "I've got the food stuff

under control now, but it wasn't always easy. How's everything else going?"

"Okay. Though it's such a pain having to take my insulin at school and having to monitor my blood sugar at school and at football. I hate drawing so much attention to myself. It's the same with lunch. I know it's not the worst thing in the world, but I've been bringing my lunch to school until I get the hang of planning my meals. I miss the hot lunches, and no one else I know brings. It makes me feel like such a dork. You know what I mean?"

"Actually, I bring lunch a lot just cuz I like my mom's food," Roger said.

Tim felt like he'd put his foot in his mouth. It *figured* Roger brought his lunch. But Roger didn't seem fazed by Tim's comment.

"Of course, I pack my *own* lunches now," Roger continued. "My mom and dad had a little too much fun writing notes and drawing things on my lunch bags. It got to be a little embarrassing."

"You? Embarrassed?" Tim blurted. He hadn't meant anything by it, but Roger blushed.

"You wouldn't think I'd get embarrassed all that easily!" Roger said. "I don't, really. But, I mean, wouldn't *anyone* be embarrassed if their mom drew a cartoon elephant on their lunch bag? We're thirteen, for crying out loud!"

Tim laughed. That *would* be embarrassing.

"But I remember what it was like at first, having trouble figuring out what to eat," Roger went on. "It'll get easier to start buying lunch. It did for me. And I know what you mean about the insulin and checking your blood sugar at school. When I was diagnosed, I was seven, and—"

"*Seven?*" Tim asked. "That's so young!"

"Yeah," Roger said. "It was pretty crazy. I

mean, I couldn't even check my blood sugar by myself at that age. I had to have a school nurse help with everything."

"Geez, and I thought I had it hard," Tim said.

"Well, we each experience things in our own way," said Roger, sounding particularly world-weary. "I'm sure what I went through was no harder than what you're going through now. The good thing about getting diagnosed so young was that my parents really took care of everything for me, at least for a while. Learning how to handle my diabetes became second nature because I almost didn't know any different. Plus I didn't have to worry about what anyone else thought at school because we were all just little kids. Actually, I remember some kids being jealous because of the extra attention I got." Roger chuckled.

"No kidding," said Tim.

"Did you tell your friends about your diabetes?" Roger asked. "I know for some kids it takes a while."

"Yeah, they all know," Tim said. "But I don't like to talk about it with them that much. They can't really understand, you know?"

"Do they ask you about it?" Roger asked.

"Sometimes," said Tim.

"Sounds like you've got some nice friends. My friends are great about my diabetes. They know just as much about it as I do, practically." Roger laughed. "Of course, it doesn't hurt that I hardly ever stop talking. They don't really have a choice in the matter! But seriously, they're awesome. Whenever we have chess tournaments or whatever—most of my friends play chess with me—they always bring snacks they know I can easily work in, that kind of thing. It's pretty nice."

"My friends all live for fast food," said Tim.

"Have you tried Burger Heaven?" asked Roger. "The food's great and they list all of their nutritional information. Plus, they have some great healthy options if that's what you want."

"Well, my friends really love Burger Joint," said Tim. "I just don't see them changing restaurants."

"Well maybe they haven't heard about this place. It couldn't hurt to mention it," said Roger.

Tim knew Roger was right. But that would mean talking to his friends about his diabetes. And he really wasn't up for that.

Tim smiled at Roger. He seemed like a good guy. Yes, he was goofy, but he was also pretty funny, in his own way. Tim wished he could be as bold as Roger from time to time. Maybe hanging out with him would be good for Tim—aside from just having someone to talk to about his type 1 diabetes.

"Hey, man, this was great," Tim said as they packed up their stuff and got ready to head home. "We should do this again some-time."

"That would be awesome!" Roger exclaimed, waving his gangly arms in the air. "There's so much more we can talk about!"

Tim chuckled. "Absolutely," he said as the two walked out the door.

Chapter 8

The bell rang after seventh period. Usually, the middle schoolers had eight periods, but this was no ordinary day. Today was the second Friday of the school year—and the first football game of the season. At Haddon Middle School, that was cause for a pep rally. Tim could hardly wait.

Tim met up with Hank by their lockers, and the two waded through the throng of students heading to the gymnasium. As they filed into the gym, Tim and Hank found the rest of their teammates seated in the front rows of the bleachers toward the back of the room.

Tim greeted his friends. Sam and a few of the other guys seemed distracted, talking and laughing loudly to one another and watching the cheerleaders.

Tim spotted Jenny Kingston among the cheerleaders. Jenny was in his homeroom. She was one of the nicest girls at school, although Tim didn't know her very well.

Jenny caught Tim's eye and smiled.

Whoa, thought Tim. *Did she just smile at me?* Tim had always thought Jenny was kind of cute. But maybe it was just an accident that she smiled at him.

Principal Groban coughed into the microphone, snapping Tim out of his thoughts. "Ahem," he said. "Attention, please. Let's get this pep rally under way."

The students quieted down a bit. "Welcome to the first pep rally of the year," Principal Groban said. "As all of you know, football is an institution in this town, and we at Haddon Middle School take great pride in our football team. To begin, I'd like everyone to join me in singing our school fight song."

Three hundred kids' voices—not always in tune—began to sing the Hornets' fight song, which included a lot of buzzing like a bee. Tim always got a kick out of how cheesy it was.

When the song was over, Principal Groban invited Coach Purcell to the podium to give a speech. "It is an honor to be speaking to you today, and we can't wait to have your support on the field tonight. The Grier City Greyhounds are a tough team, that's for sure."

This was followed by a round of boos from the audience, led by Sam and the football team.

"But we've been training hard, and we're ready to show them what we've got. The Haddon Hornets are as solid as ever. Team, why don't you stand up so your school can recognize you?"

Tim and his teammates stood to a chorus of cheers from the students. Tim was proud of his team. He couldn't wait to join them on the field that night.

After a performance by the cheerleaders, the students began to gather their things to exit school for the day. Suddenly, Tim saw Roger. He was wearing a yellow-and-black striped hat with bee antennae. Well, at least he has school spirit, Tim thought to himself.

"Hey, dude-man," said Roger. "You must be so excited for tonight! I just wanted to say good luck!" Roger high-fived Tim. *Who high-fives anymore?* thought Tim, but he obliged anyway.

"Thanks, Roger," Tim said. He looked

around to see if anyone else had noticed the two of them talking, but all his buddies seemed distracted. He turned back to Roger. "You coming tonight?" he asked.

"You bet!" Roger said. "My chess buddies aren't much into football, but I talked them into coming so you'd have an extra-geeky cheering section."

"Well, that was really nice of you," said Tim. "I'll give you a wave from the sidelines if I can find you."

"Oh, you'll be able to spot us," Roger said. "I got the whole group these hilarious hats to wear tonight! You won't be able to miss us!"

Tim laughed awkwardly. Great. That was just the attention he needed. Right then, Sam walked past the two of them. Sam chuckled derisively. "Nice hat, dorkwad," he said to Roger, continuing on his way.

Tim's face turned beet red. "Don't worry

about him," said Tim. "He doesn't know what he's talking about."

For a moment, Roger looked crestfallen, but he recovered quickly. "No biggie," he said. "That's the price you pay for being unique! Anyway, I'd better let you get back to your friends. See you tonight!"

"See ya," Tim said. He felt terrible. Why did Sam have to say stuff like that? But he also felt a little ashamed, because a tiny part of him felt embarrassed to be talking to Roger in the first place.

"What did that guy want?" Hank asked, friendly enough.

Tim felt his face turn bright red. Hank might be his best friend, but that didn't mean Tim wanted him to know he was hanging out with one of the less-cool kids at school — especially someone as goofy as Roger.

"Who, that guy? Roger?" Tim asked, acting clueless.

"Is that his name?" Hank asked.

"Uh, yeah," Tim stammered. "He's just a guy from one of my classes. He wanted to wish me good luck. I don't know why. I hardly know him."

Hank just shrugged.

Tim paused. Why was he holding back the truth from his best friend? Wouldn't Hank of all people understand if he wanted to be friends with someone who could relate to what he was going through? But Roger was a dork. Or at least that's what everyone said about him. When it came down to it, Tim was embarrassed by Roger, and he just didn't want Hank to know they were friends.

Chapter 9

Tim pulled on his padding, his jersey, and his cleats, and then grabbed his helmet out of the top of his locker. He took a deep breath and looked around at his teammates, all seemingly relaxed and joking with one another. This was Tim's first football game with diabetes. He was nervous, but he knew he was as prepared as he could be. He had met with his diabetes nurse after school the day before, and they'd developed a plan for the game. He had already had a snack and checked his blood sugar. He just hoped his playing would hold up.

Finally it was time to head out to the field.

"You ready?" asked Hank.

"You bet," Tim said with a smile. Nervousness aside, he was excited to play again.

They exited the locker room, and Tim heard the cheers coming from the crowd. As they approached the field, the noise in the stadium grew louder.

At the announcer's cue, the entire Hornets football team—led by Henry—ran out onto the field. The home-team cheers overwhelmed the boos from the visiting team's fans.

Tim took his position, and the first play got under way. He successfully covered the Greyhounds' wide receiver. After the play, Tim looked up to see his mom and

Kayla cheering in the stands. Tim smiled and waved. Just a few feet from them, Tim saw a blur of yellow and black. It was Roger and his friends in their bee hats. They were shouting and yelling excitedly. Roger was waving, too. A little embarrassed, Tim raised his hand and gave them a half-smile.

"Geez, what are those dorks going so nuts about?" asked Dale, the team defensive end, who Tim suddenly found standing next to him. Tim wasn't great friends with Dale, but he respected and liked him. Which made it all the more humiliating that he thought Roger and his friends were being weird.

Dale laughed lightheartedly, but Tim felt a flush rise into his face. Had Dale seen him wave to Roger and his friends? He didn't think so; otherwise, Dale probably wouldn't have said anything to him. Ugh. Tim wished Roger and his friends would just chill out!

By halftime, the score was 14–14. Tim had missed a couple of key plays, allowing the Greyhounds' receiver to catch the ball twice. Luckily, Haddon's safeties stopped him from scoring each time. Tim was upset about his mistakes, but he knew he had to move on and do his best to recover from them.

The team made its way to the locker room, where Coach Purcell spent halftime running through the plays for the final half. As Tim stood up to head back out to the field, he noticed that he felt a little woozy. A cold sweat had broken out on his face, neck, and arms. He started to feel shaky and weak.

"Tim?" he heard a voice ask. It sounded like Hank. "You okay?"

Tim nodded. "I think I'm low. I need to check my blood sugar."

He couldn't believe this was happening again. And at a game! Tim reached into his locker and took out his glucose meter. Sure enough, his blood sugar was low. Tim pulled a bottle of glucose tablets out of his bag and took a few.

"I hate to say it," said Coach Purcell, "but I think it's best if you sit out the start of the third quarter, rest up, and get better." Tim's heart sank. "After that, we'll evaluate where your blood sugar is at and see if we can get you back out there."

"Okay," Tim said reluctantly, slowly sipping some water he'd taken out of his bag. He knew he'd need some time for his glucose tablets to take effect. Sitting out was his only choice. He'd recheck his level in fifteen minutes and see if he was ready to play again.

Tim followed the team back out to the field and took a seat on the bench. As he watched the scoreless third quarter, he found that he was feeling better. The symptoms of low blood sugar had subsided.

With a few minutes left in the quarter, Tim checked his blood sugar. Everything was back within target range. He had a quick snack to keep his level up and talked to Coach Purcell, who gave him the okay to get back out on the field.

Tim powered through the final quarter of the game as best he could, the Hornets barely squeaking out a win against the Greyhounds with a score of 24–21. Tim fist-bumped his teammates, and the other team congratulated them on a game well played. As the Hornets walked off the field, Joe asked, "So who wants to go out for a celebratory meal?"

"Sounds great, man," said Sam. "How about we go to Burger Joint?"

A few guys chimed in their agreement.

Tim didn't say anything. Eating out after the game had not been part of the plan he and his diabetes nurse had come up with. If Tim had been able to plan ahead, if he'd known he would have to bring his insulin to the game and figure out how to work in the fast food, that would have been one thing. But now he just felt stuck.

Tim thought about saying something, but he decided not to. They wouldn't be out late. He could just hang out and then eat dinner at home, like he'd planned.

At Burger Joint, Tim sat down with his teammates, who filled a few adjacent booths. The waitress soon came by and passed out menus to each of them. Tim opened his and stared at it blankly. It turned out there was a side salad on the menu. At least he could eat that.

The waitress came by and took their order.

"I'll have the side salad and a diet cola," Tim said.

"Geez, Tim, you're eating like a little girl," said Sam with a laugh. "Worried about your weight or something?"

"No, nothing like that," Tim said.

"He just has to be careful because of his diabetes," Hank chimed in.

Grateful, Tim smiled at his friend.

"Oh, I got it," said Sam. "Sorry, dude."

"No problem," Tim said.

While they waited for their food to arrive, Tim kept to himself. He had felt so pumped after the game, but now he was feeling a little bummed. He couldn't believe he'd had to sit out almost a whole quarter! And now he couldn't even eat a meal with his friends.

"Hey, did you guys see those geeks in the stands with bee hats on?" Sam said. "I mean, it's cool to come out and cheer, but you don't have to act like a little kid."

The guys laughed. Tim just stared at Sam. Should he say something?

"Yeah, they looked ridiculous," said Joe.

"How embarrassing," Hank said.

"It was nice that they came out to support the team, though, right?" Tim said, trying to put a positive spin on the discussion.

Sam shrugged. "I guess," he said. "Though I'd rather have cool kids rooting for me instead of losers."

Tim looked down. He didn't know what to say. None of the guys even knew he was friends with Roger. If he kept on defending him, they might think something was up.

Finally, the food arrived. Tim salivated over his friends' meals as he picked at his boring salad. He wished he'd been able to plan ahead so he could order a burger, like his friends. He missed the days of being able to eat whatever he wanted without a second thought. Right now he wished he had never been diagnosed with type 1 diabetes. It made life so much more complicated.

Chapter 10

The following Monday after football practice, Tim and Roger met at the Koffee Klatch again.

"Thanks again for coming to the game," Tim said. "It was really nice to have my own cheering section." Tim smiled. Although he had been embarrassed at the time, he had realized over the weekend what a nice gesture it was for Roger to get his friends out there to cheer for him.

"Oh, it was nothing!" Roger said. "I think my buddies had a good time. They may not be into football, but those guys were way into the popcorn and hot chocolate." Roger chuckled. "Oh, hey, Jen!"

Tim looked up to see Jenny Kingston at the coffee shop counter, placing an order for herself. An overstuffed backpack hung over her shoulders.

At the sound of Roger's voice, Jenny turned and waved. "Hey, Tim. Hey, Roger," she said as she walked over with her iced tea. "What are you guys up to?"

"Just hanging out," said Roger. "You here to study for algebra?"

Tim had no idea that Jenny was on the fast track for math. Most eighth graders took regular math, but a handful took the advanced algebra class.

"Yeah," she said. "I'm meeting Kim Rhee here. Are you ready for the quiz?"

"I think so," said Roger.

Just then, Kim walked in the door.

"Guess I'd better go," Jenny said sweetly. "Talk to you guys later!"

Jenny walked off, and Tim realized that he hadn't said a single word to her the entire time she'd been there. He felt silly. Why had he been so quiet?

"She's super nice, huh?" said Roger mindlessly, sipping his hot chocolate.

"Yeah," said Tim, feeling a blush cover his face. "I had no idea you two were friends."

"Most of the cheerleaders won't give me the time of day," said Roger, "but she's always been pretty cool."

"Hey," Roger continued, "I've been thinking. I go to this diabetes group every couple of weeks. It's through the Haddon community center, downtown. Anyway, it's for middle school kids with type 1 diabetes in Haddon and the surrounding area. It gives us a chance to get together and hang out. Do you want to come sometime?"

Tim hesitated. "Uh. What do you do there?" he asked. He imagined a group of Roger clones sitting around talking enthusiastically about insulin doses and blood sugar levels.

"Oh, it's really casual!" Roger said. "We just get together and hang out, play games, talk, go out to eat, that kind of thing. There are a handful of people who come to each meeting. I've made some really neat friends that way."

"I don't know," said Tim. "I've got enough friends already."

Roger looked a bit slighted at Tim's comment. "They're really normal kids," said Roger. "They're not weird or anything. They're just like you and me."

"I know," Tim said. It just sounded sort of nerdy to him. A "support" group? Wasn't that for people who had real problems? "I just don't think I need it," he continued. "I'm doing fine on my own."

"Okay," said Roger. "I'm not going to force the idea or anything. But it's made me a lot happier having a group of people to hang out with who really get what I'm going through. It's nice to have a reminder now and then that you're not alone."

"I guess," Tim said. "Maybe I'll just go to one meeting to see what it's like."

"Thatta boy!" said Roger, a grin spreading across his face, his goofiness back in full force. "Our next meeting is Sunday afternoon. You won't regret it!"

Chapter 11

On Sunday, Tim's mom dropped him off at the community center for the diabetes group. As the car pulled up, Tim spotted Roger and a couple of other kids milling about in front of the entrance.

"Hola, Tim-bo!" Roger exclaimed. He was standing next to a small blond girl and a boy who was about as tall as Roger, but much more muscular.

"This is Lola," Roger said, introducing

Tim to the girl, "and this is Ricky. Lola, Ricky, this is Tim."

"Should we head inside?" Lola asked, her voice somewhat squeaky.

Tim nodded and followed the others down a hallway to a rec room. Three other people Tim's age were already there.

Tim, Roger, Lola, and Ricky joined the others in the circle of couches. When they were settled, Roger introduced Tim to Amy, Seth, and Johanna, all of whom seemed really nice.

Tim quickly learned that the kids were from middle schools all around the region. Apparently, this was one of the only groups like it anywhere in the area, and some of the kids drove at least an hour just to get there.

"So, Tim, how's it been going?" asked Seth, a redhead with a nose full of freckles.

"Okay," Tim said. "Taking care of my diabetes at school has been kind of a hassle, but I'm getting the hang of it."

"I know what you mean," said Ricky. "I hate having to ask for permission to leave class every time I want to check my blood sugar."

Tim's ears perked up. He had been having the exact same problem. By asking to leave class to check his blood sugar, he was drawing attention to himself—the exact opposite of what he wanted to do.

"Wait," said Amy, her long mane of strawberry-blond hair bouncing as she talked. "You have to ask permission every time you leave the room?"

Ricky nodded.

"Why don't you just talk to your teachers about it?" Amy said. "That's what I did. They agreed to let me have a special hall pass that I can use anytime I want to go down to the nurse's office. I don't even have to ask to leave."

"That's a really good idea," said Tim. "I think I might try that, too."

As Tim looked around at the group, he realized how comfortable he felt. Everyone was so nice. They seemed genuinely happy to have him there, and it put him right at ease. And it was nice that the one thing he'd been trying to keep to himself—his diabetes— could be talked about openly and totally understood by a whole group of people.

But the most surprising thing to Tim was that the conversation wasn't dominated entirely by discussions about diabetes-related stuff. They talked about sports, school, movies, and TV. They really were just normal people. Tim wasn't sure what he had expected—maybe that they'd spend the whole time gushing their deepest, darkest diabetes thoughts—but it was a whole lot better than he thought it would be.

After talking for a while, people split off to play pool and card games.

"Do you want to play air hockey?" Ricky asked Tim.

Tim readily agreed. The two took their positions at the air hockey table and began batting away at the puck.

"So, you play football, Tim?" Ricky asked.

"Yep!" Tim replied. "I play cornerback. I even get to start this year."

"Me too," said Ricky. "I play football, I mean. I'm a defensive lineman for Princeville. But we aren't in your division, so we wouldn't play each other."

"Oh, cool," said Tim. Princeville was always going to the state championship for its division. A much smaller one than Haddon's, Ricky's division was mostly made up of private schools.

"Isn't it a pain having to check your blood

sugar during games and stuff?" Ricky asked.

"Not really," Tim said. "My coach has been really encouraging. All my teammates know about my diabetes, but it is a little awkward because they don't understand that much about it. So, like, they always decide they want to eat out at the last minute. It's hard to plan around."

Ding! Tim scored a goal on Ricky's end of the table.

"Nice job," Ricky said. "Why don't you say something to your teammates? Fill them in a little bit here and there about what it means to have type 1 diabetes."

"I just don't think they'd care," said Tim. "And I don't want them to think I have any distractions from football."

"I can respect that last part, but I'm sure they care more than you think. They're your friends, right?"

"Yeah," Tim said. He let his mind drift as

the two continued to battle over their game of air hockey. Tim scored twice more and Ricky put up one point.

"I don't mean to be pushy or anything," Ricky said as he scored another point on Tim. "I just think you'd be a lot more comfortable if you didn't try to hold back. I think your friends would probably like to know more. I know mine are always, like, really interested in learning more about diabetes. I think sometimes people just don't know how to ask about it, so you have to be the one to fill them in."

Tim thought about that. "You're probably right," he said. "I'd probably feel weird asking my friend about his diabetes if he never talked about it. I'd worry it was something he didn't *want* to talk about, so I should just leave it alone."

"That's what I think," said Ricky. "Anyway, give it some thought."

By the time Ricky and Tim finished their game, it was time for everyone to go home.

"Hey, Tim," Roger said. "Can I catch a ride home with you? My dad had to work the night shift, so he can't come get me."

"Sure," Tim agreed.

Tim's mom and Kayla were both waiting in the car when Tim and Roger got outside. Tim's mom was ecstatic to meet Roger. "I've heard so much about you!" she said. "It's nice to finally meet you."

"You too, ma'am," said Roger, his manners impeccable.

"Hi, Roger, I'm Kayla," said Tim's sister, sticking out her hand to greet him.

"Hello, Miss Kayla," said Roger. "What a pleasure to meet you!"

Kayla giggled.

"Oh, I wanted to tell you," Roger said to Tim, "we have a chess match tomorrow night. If you're not busy after practice, do you want to come by? You can meet my friends."

"Sure, that'd be great," Tim said. He was enjoying hanging out with Roger. It was more than just diabetes they had in common, after all.

"Awesome," Roger said. "You can even wear my bee hat if you want. You know, to show your support for the Hornets chess team."

Tim laughed. "No, thanks," he said. He thought back to Sam mocking Roger and his friends for wearing them to the football game. "The bee hats are awesome, but they're not really my style."

"That's cool," Roger said and turned to talk to Kayla.

As Tim listened to his friend and his sister talk about their favorite music, his mind wandered. He couldn't believe he'd agreed to go to Roger's chess match. What would his friends say if they found out about it? Would

Sam call him a dork, like he did Roger, and refuse to hang out with him? Roger was nice and all, but was he worth losing his other friends over?

Chapter 12

Later that week, Hank was over at Tim's house, playing video games. Tim was pressing the buttons on his controller furiously, struggling to keep up with Hank's score. Hank spent all his free time gaming, so Tim was used to getting his butt kicked.

"I cannot believe the game against the Bears is in two weeks," said Tim.

"Tell me about it," Hank replied. "At least they're never any good."

The Briarwood Middle School Bears—Haddon's rivals—were notorious for their losing streaks. Tim felt for them. But Hank was right; at least it would make for an easy win.

"By the way," Hank said as he continued to play the video game. "Nice job at practice today. Joe couldn't get open with your coverage."

"Thanks." Tim had to admit, he had been feeling better at practice this week. "Maybe Sam will stop heckling me now," he said, laughing.

"Don't count on it," Hank said with a grin. Sam's tendency to pick on people—even his own friends—could be wearing at times, but they knew at the end of the day that he was their friend. Tim just wished he'd lay off Roger.

As if he had read Tim's mind, Hank said, "So what's up with you hanging out with that

Roger guy?" Hank's eyes were still on the screen as he spoke.

Tim was surprised Hank knew they were friends. He'd never mentioned Roger to his best friend before.

"My dad and I stopped to pick up hot chocolate at the Koffee Klatch, and you guys were sitting in a booth. You looked busy, so I didn't bother you."

Tim lifted his eyes from the TV and glanced over at Hank. He didn't seem bothered by it or anything, Tim noticed, just curious.

Tim thought for a moment before answering. He didn't want to spill any personal information about Roger without his permission, but Hank *was* his best friend. And Roger was pretty open about his diabetes.

"He's got type 1 diabetes, like me," Tim said finally.

"Oh," Hank answered, like he wasn't sure what to say.

"The school nurse suggested we hang out. I wasn't sure at first, but my mom kind of made me," Tim lied. "So we just meet up now and then."

"Huh, I see," said Hank. "Well, that guy seems kind of weird."

Tim shrugged, feeling a little bit defensive about Roger. He had gotten to know him pretty well, lately, after all. Roger was a lot of fun, and he was really nice. He didn't deserve the bad rap he got. "Yeah. He's actually a pretty good guy. You'd probably like him."

"Yeah," Hank said. "You're probably right."

"Do you want to hang out with us sometime?" Tim asked.

"I dunno," said Hank. "No offense, but I don't think he's my kind of guy."

Tim was surprised by Hank's response. Usually he was really easygoing about stuff like this. Maybe Sam and the pressure to fit in at school were getting to him, too. Tim let the topic go at that.

"How's everything going with your diabetes, anyway?" said Hank. "If you want to talk about it, that is."

Tim hesitated. But then he thought about what Ricky had said about sharing with his friends. Not that he was about to tell Hank he was in a diabetes group. But maybe he could fill him in a little bit.

"It's okay," said Tim. "I'm finally getting good at counting carbs, so maybe I can start buying lunch again soon. And I'm adjusting to my school schedule, too."

"What do you mean?" Hank asked. He paused the game and looked up at Tim.

"Just, you know, I have to go take my insulin in the nurse's office before lunch, for one thing. And I've been going there whenever I want to check my blood sugar, too. Sometimes I have to leave in the middle of class, if I feel like I might be having a low."

"Oh, wow," said Hank. "I didn't know that. How do you get out of class for that?"

Tim smiled. "Actually, I got a special hall pass so that I can leave to check my blood sugar whenever I want," he said. He had followed Amy's advice and talked to his teachers about it. They were more than happy to oblige, and Tim was thankful for the idea.

"Oh, well, that's pretty cool," said Hank. "I wish I had a hall pass for whenever I want to leave class—which is, like, always!" he said with a laugh.

"No kidding," said Tim. "Except I wish I was leaving class to go somewhere cool, instead of to the nurse's office. I mean Nurse Swanski's nice and all, but I'd rather be going for frozen yogurt or something."

Hank laughed. "Yeah, I get that. So, like, are you getting used to having diabetes?"

Tim laughed. "Kind of? I don't know.

Sometimes I think I'm getting the hang of it, and then something will happen, like I'll get a low, like at that first football practice. Or I'm not sure what to eat because I don't know how many carbs are in the food. Hopefully it'll start to feel normal sometime soon. But I'm not really there yet."

"Oh," said Hank. "That's rough. It seems like you got diagnosed forever ago."

"It feels like that to me sometimes, too, and other times it feels like it was just yesterday. Anyway, it's cool that you asked about it," Tim said.

"Sure, dude," said Hank.

Tim and Hank went back to focusing on their video game, but Tim felt as if a little weight had been lifted off his chest. Maybe he hadn't been giving his best friend enough credit.

Chapter 13

The next Wednesday after football practice, Tim was at Sammy's Subs, waiting for Roger to show up. Tim hadn't particularly wanted to meet Roger there. His football friends loved to come to Sammy's for meatball subs after practice, and he was sure Sam would heckle him if he showed up and saw Tim hanging out with Roger.

Tim's thoughts were interrupted when Roger suddenly burst through the door.

"Hey, Tim-bo," Roger said. Tim couldn't believe it, but he was actually getting used to that nickname. In fact, it was starting to grow on him.

Tim and Roger each got a soda.

As they drank, Roger taught Tim how to play chess. Tim had been nervous about going to Roger's match, and had been pleasantly surprised to find that the game actually looked kind of fun. Roger had happily agreed to teach him.

"Chess is actually like football," Roger began.

Tim looked at Roger as if he were crazy, and Roger laughed.

"No, I mean it!" he said. "Chess and football are all about being mentally prepared to play. They're both all about tactics, and guessing what your opponent's next step will be."

"Huh," Tim said. He never would have

thought of it that way before. But as they began playing, Tim realized it was kind of true. Sure, football was a far more physical sport, but they both required the same kind of thinking to get ahead.

"Checkmate!" Roger shouted, doing a dance around the table.

Tim laughed. Roger might not be very popular, but he was definitely fun to hang out with.

Roger stopped dancing and looked down at his watch. "Man, I'd better get outta here," he said. "I'm gonna be late for tutoring!"

Tim shook his head. Funny *and* smart. Roger was only in eighth grade, but he was tutoring *ninth* graders in math.

As Roger walked toward the door, Tim heard a voice call his name. He looked up to see Sam, Joe, and Henry walking into the sub shop.

"Hey, buddy," said Sam. "I just saw that

weirdo Roger walk out of here. Was he waving at *you*? Did I miss the memo? Are you two friends or something?"

Tim paused. His friendship with Roger was supposed to be a secret. Finally he said, "No way, man! You think I hang out with nerds?"

But as he said it, he realized that Roger wasn't quite out of earshot. And it looked like he'd heard every word Tim had said.

Sam snickered, nudging Tim in the chest as he scooted into the booth next to him. Tim ignored him.

"You okay?" Henry asked, noticing Tim's downcast face.

"I'm fine," Tim said. "Just, you know, have some studying to do."

"Man, you study a lot!" Joe said with a laugh. "You'd think with all the time we spend together, you'd be a better influence on me."

Tim laughed. As the guys sat around shooting the breeze, talking about next week's homecoming game against the Bears, Tim forgot all about Roger.

Chapter 14

The next night, Tim followed the scent of his mom's signature lasagna into the kitchen. It smelled amazing. Kayla was busy setting the table.

"Hey, Timmy!" she said. "How's it going?"

"It's all right," said Tim. "How was school today?" ·

"Awesome, as always!" Kayla exclaimed. "Omigosh, I love middle school, Tim! It's so much fun."

Tim laughed, pulling out a chair and sitting down. Leave it to his sis to find sixth grade, in his opinion the toughest year of middle school, to be a ton of fun.

Tim's mom joined them at the table. As they started eating, they caught up on one another's days.

"How's Roger doing?" Tim's mom asked.

"He's good, I guess," said Tim. Actually, Tim hadn't talked to Roger at all today. He just felt awkward after the scene at Sammy's Subs, and he had the sinking suspicion that Roger might be avoiding him.

"Actually . . ." Tim began, "I'm not sure how he is. I think he's mad at me."

"Mad at you?" Tim's mom said. "Why?"

Tim was too embarrassed to admit to his mother that Roger had overheard Tim calling him a nerd. He knew how terrible it was. "I just . . . said something stupid. I think I hurt his feelings. Roger's just . . . not like me.

He plays chess instead of football. He's really into school and I'm not. He's super goofy and I'm just . . . normal."

"Tim, that's so mean!" Kayla said. "Roger's normal, too. And why do all your friends have to be football players anyway? That doesn't make them automatically cool."

"Sure, it does," Tim said.

Kayla rolled her eyes at him.

"At Haddon Middle School it does," he protested.

"Oh, Tim," said his mother, sounding disappointed. "School is not the end all, be all. Neither is popularity. Roger has been so good to you. Why does it matter if he's not 'cool' like you are?"

Tim sighed. "I don't know," he said. "My friends think he's a nerd. I guess I'm embarrassed to hang out with him because I don't want them to think I'm a nerd, too."

"You should be friends with who you want

to be friends with," Kayla said. "It doesn't matter what your football buddies think. If they're your real friends, it won't matter."

"Kayla's right," said Tim's mom. "Roger has been a good friend to you, and it sounds like maybe you aren't returning the favor. He's a nice person. He doesn't judge you for who *you* are, does he?"

Tim shook his head. "No, of course not."

"Yeah," Kayla said, crossing her arms across her chest. "Cuz Roger's awesome."

"Well, if he can accept you for who you are, why can't you just accept him for who *he* is, too?" asked his mother.

Tim sighed again. If only it were so simple.

Chapter 15

The next day at school, Tim found Roger in the hallway by his locker, unloading a backpack stuffed with books.

"Hey," Roger said cautiously, looking up. He was obviously still a little bothered by Tim's dismissal of him the other night. But at least he wasn't avoiding Tim anymore.

"Hi, Roger," Tim said. "Look, I'm sorry about what I said the other day. It wasn't cool. And it wasn't true. You're one of the best guys I know. I just wish I could make my friends realize that."

Roger sighed and looked down. "Look," he said. "I get it. You're embarrassed by me. I'm not as cool as your football friends. That's not exactly news to me, but I thought we were friends. And seriously, man, if you can't stand up to your friends and tell them the truth, then maybe we shouldn't be friends anymore."

Roger had barely looked at Tim the whole time he spoke. Tim felt terrible, like his heart had sunk down into his stomach, like his feet were made of concrete. He thought about what his mom and Kayla had said last night, about accepting Roger for who he was. They were right. This was not how he wanted things to go. But he wasn't ready to tell Sam and the other football guys to lay off Roger. He didn't want to make them mad, to make them treat *him* like they did Roger.

"I have a lot of fun with you, Roger," Tim said finally, "but I don't want to cause a mess with my friends. I'm sorry."

For a second, Roger looked shocked. Then, suddenly, he looked cool and distant. He casually threw his backpack over his shoulder. "It's fine. See you around," he said, walking off. Roger acted like he couldn't care less, but Tim knew he'd hurt his friend. Or, his ex-friend, anyway. He'd never felt more terrible in his life.

A couple of days later, Tim was in Nurse Swanski's office getting his insulin.

"So, how are you adjusting to handling your diabetes at school?" Nurse Swanski asked. "Things have been so busy around here, I haven't had the chance to ask you about it much since school started."

"Oh, they're fine," said Tim. "I'm starting to get the hang of things."

"I'm so glad to hear it," said Nurse Swanski. "Did you ever wind up giving Roger Jablonski a call? Such a nice boy, that one."

Tim gave himself his insulin, trying to take his time while he figured out how to respond.

"Uh, yeah," he finally managed. "I did." He didn't want to say anything else about it. He hoped Nurse Swanski wouldn't ask anything else.

"Oh good!" Nurse Swanski said, beaming. "Was he helpful to you?"

Tim shrugged, standing up and getting his bag. He couldn't wait to get out of there all of a sudden. "Yeah," he said, looking at the ground as he spoke and shuffling his feet nervously. "Thanks for, um, giving me his number."

"You in a hurry to get out of here today?" asked Nurse Swanski. "You must be hungry for lunch or something."

"Kind of," said Tim. "I'll see you tomorrow."

"All right," Nurse Swanski said. "See you then."

Tim couldn't rush out of the nurse's office fast enough. What he didn't tell Nurse Swanski, what he was barely able to admit to himself, was that while Roger had been an enormous help to Tim, Tim had returned the favor by turning his back on Roger. Roger *was* a nice guy, like Nurse Swanski said. Tim, on the other hand, felt like the biggest jerk in school.

At lunch, Tim was still feeling crummy about his conversation with Nurse Swanski. He sat quietly, eating his lunch and listening to his friends talk.

Suddenly, he spotted Roger carrying his bagged lunch past them. Roger glanced quickly over at Tim's table and looked away. But in the moment he wasn't looking in front of him, Roger tripped on the wheel of a trash can and went flying, sending the contents of his lunch bag flying.

"Oh, ho, ho!" Sam belly-laughed. "Flying nerd alert!"

The other guys joined in, laughing hysterically.

Tim jumped up from his seat and rushed over to Roger, helping him gather his things. "You okay?" he asked his dazed-looking friend.

Roger looked relieved and thankful for Tim's help. But then, as though suddenly remembering he and Tim weren't friends, his face took on a steely look.

"I'm fine," he said. "Thanks for your help." And without another word, Roger hurried out of sight. Tim watched him go, then made his way back to his lunch table.

"Why are you helping that loser?" Sam said, still laughing. "That was too funny."

"He's not a loser, and it wasn't funny," said Tim. "He could have been hurt!"

Sam shrugged. "Whatever."

Tim felt emboldened by Sam's dismissal of his friend. "You know, Roger's actually really cool and fun. He's my friend, and I'm sick of pretending he isn't."

"Your *friend*, huh?" said Sam. "I thought you said he was a nerd. Are you a nerd, too, Tim?"

Tim looked over in Hank's direction. His best friend was looking down at his food, an uncomfortable look on his face. Tim turned back to Sam.

"You know, you should hang out with him before you judge him. You don't even know him," Tim told Sam.

Sam just snorted.

"I'm sure he's nice," Henry said, trying to break through the awkwardness. "He just isn't really our kind of guy. You know?"

"You should give him a chance," said Tim. "He's been really cool to me, especially helping me out with my diabetes."

Tim looked around. His friends had gone quiet. Hank was still pretending to be too involved in eating to pay attention. Sam was texting someone. Henry shrugged at Tim, as though to say he was sorry. It seemed like there was nothing Tim could do to change his friends' minds. Finally, Hank caught Tim's eye and gave his friend a sympathetic look. But he didn't come to Tim's defense. Tim had to prove to his football friends that Roger was worth getting to know.

Chapter 16

Later that week, Tim was doing homework on the couch when his cell phone rang. It was Hank.

"Hey, Tim," Hank said. "What's up?"

"Not much," Tim replied. "Just studying for Spanish. What's going on?"

Hank took a deep breath. "I'm sorry for what happened at lunch the other day."

"What do you mean?" Tim asked.

"I should have helped you out, tried to

get the other guys to see that Roger might be worth getting to know," Hank answered. "You're my best friend. You obviously have great taste in friends."

Tim and Hank both laughed.

"But seriously, I think I just let the team get to me sometimes," Hank said. "They're the best, but they aren't always the most welcoming group. I don't think they mean to be that way. I think it's just easier sometimes."

Tim was surprised to hear his friend say this. It was exactly how he'd been feeling all along with Roger. "I know what you mean," Tim said. "To tell you the truth, I was embarrassed for a long time about hanging out with Roger. I didn't even tell you guys we were friends for a while. Sam's always picking on him, and I guess that made me think no one would understand why I was friends with him. But the truth is, it's been really nice to have a friend with diabetes to talk to. And it's more than that. He's just a good guy."

"I totally get that," said Hank. "If you want, I can talk to the other guys. See if maybe they'll give Roger a chance."

"I don't know," said Tim. "They just really didn't seem interested, and I don't want anyone to treat Roger badly. Especially Sam."

"I think he's the only one you'd need to worry about," said Hank.

"Maybe I'll have a talk with him," said Tim. "But I still don't know how to get everyone to hang out."

"What if Roger came to practice one day? You guys could talk to the team about type 1 diabetes," said Hank.

"That's not a bad idea," said Tim. "But we've got our biggest game of the season next week. We're not going to have any time to spare at practice."

"Oh, you're right," said Hank. "Maybe we can have a party or something. Invite Roger and his friends and our football friends. Just so people can hang out and get to know one another. You know, so our friends can realize that Roger's as awesome as you say he is."

"That would be so great," said Tim, feeling thankful that his friend had come around. "What if we did it after the game? Hopefully it will be a celebratory party, after we win."

"That's a good idea. Where would you have it?" Hank asked. "At your house?"

"Yeah, why not?" said Tim. "It'll just be a fun party with music and great food."

Tim was so excited, he was beginning to feel a little bit like Roger. He couldn't wait to share the idea with him.

The next day at school, Tim tracked down Roger by his locker.

"Hey," Tim said. "How's it going?"

Roger looked up, surprised to see Tim. "Oh, hey," he said. "Okay."

"You recover your pride from that spill earlier?" Tim asked, a gentle smile on his face.

Roger winced. "Yeah, I guess so," he said. "Thanks for helping me out, especially in front of your friends. I'm sure that wasn't easy for you."

Tim was amazed at how understanding Roger was being. It made him feel like an even bigger jerk.

"I told them you were my friend," Tim said. "It's stupid to pretend you're *not* my friend. And I wasn't going to just let you have some huge fall in the cafeteria and sit by and laugh. I had to help. Anyway, you were right: If my friends can't understand that you're my friend, then maybe they're not such great friends."

Roger looked hopeful. "You mean it?" he asked.

"Absolutely," Tim said. "I was being an idiot. I'm sorry I was so crummy to you. You deserve a way better friend than that. My football friends—just because people think they're cool doesn't mean they are any better than anyone else, especially you. Friends again?" Tim asked, holding out his hand.

Roger heartily shook Tim's hand. "Absolutely," he said.

"I was actually thinking there might be a way to get my football friends and our diabetes group friends and you and your chess buddies together, just to hang and get to know one another," Tim continued. "I was thinking I'd have a party at my house after the big game. We can hang out, talk, listen to music, whatever."

"Are you sure?" said Roger. "But Sam . . ."

"Don't worry about Sam," Tim said, mustering up his courage. "I'm having a talk with him. He's been getting to me lately, too. Someone needs to set him straight about how to treat other people."

"Wow," said Roger, who looked truly touched. "Thanks! Let me know how your talk with Sam goes. Gosh. I can't wait for next week!"

After practice that night, Tim pulled Sam aside in the locker room. "Can I talk to you for a sec?" he asked bravely. It hadn't been easy to work up the nerve to confront Sam about the way he'd been treating Roger . . . and Tim, for that matter.

"Sure, man, what's up?" asked Sam.

"Look, I don't want you to take this the wrong way," said Tim. "But sometimes you can be kind of judgmental about people, and I . . ."

"Wait, wait, wait," said Sam. "Is this about your diabetes? Look, man, I've been thinking about that a lot lately. I've been a real jerk to you, and I feel really bad about it. I'm sorry. I just don't know anything about it, and I didn't mean to be, well, mean to you. Truth be told, I was a little jealous of all the attention you got from everyone on the team. I hope this doesn't come out wrong, but I'm used to being the center of attention, you know?"

At that, Tim had to laugh. It reminded him of what Roger said about how when he was diagnosed at seven, other kids were jealous of the attention he got. Tim supposed that Sam was pretty immature, himself.

"It's okay," said Tim. "I really appreciate that. But it's not just me. It's Roger. You've picked on him for a while. It's not cool how you pick on kids. Roger's my friend, and I'd really appreciate it if you lay off."

"Pick on people?" said Sam. It was as though the thought had never occurred to him. "Dude, I'm just messing around."

"A lot of people don't feel that way," said Tim. "Look, you're one of the most popular kids at school. Everyone wants to be friends with you. So when you call people names, even if you think you're joking, they take it seriously."

"Really?" asked Sam. "You think I'm one of the most popular kids in school?"

"That's not the point!" said Tim, exasperated that Sam was making the conversation all about him. "You should really think about watching what you say to people."

"Whoa, man, whoa," said Sam. "I hear you loud and clear. Look, I'll work on it. And I promise to lay off Roger, okay?"

Tim supposed that was the best he could hope for . . . for now.

"Thanks," he said. "Now, I have a favor to ask of you."

"What's up?" asked Sam.

"I need you to get the guys to want to meet Roger, to get to know him. I think the reason they're holding back is because of you. They think it'll be uncool if they hang out with him."

"Well, that's cuz he's a dork."

"Sam!" said Tim.

"Sorry!" Sam replied. "Old habits. I can do that for you. But do you really think I'm the reason they don't want to get to know Roger?"

"I'm sure of it," Tim said. "I didn't even want to tell you guys we were friends at first because I was afraid of what you would think."

This seemed to strike a chord with Sam. "Wow," he said. "I had no idea. All right, I'll talk to them."

"It means a lot," said Tim, smiling at his friend. Tim knew Sam wouldn't change overnight, but at least things seemed to be heading in the right direction.

Chapter 17

The day of the game finally arrived. Haddon Middle School had kicked off the day's events with another pep rally in the gymnasium, and the team was feeling pumped. Now, hours later, Tim and the rest of the defense stood on the sidelines as the offense took the field. The fall air was chilly, but you wouldn't know it by looking at the football team, sweating in their short-sleeved uniforms.

The game was neck and neck. The Briarwood Middle School Bears were a surprisingly tough opponent. Haddon had thought they would have an easy game. Boy, were they wrong! For each field goal or touchdown Haddon scored, the Bears roared back with one of their own. The score was currently tied, 24–24, with just two minutes left in the game.

Tim really wanted to win. Not only would it be great for the team, but it would be the perfect lead-in to the party later. He looked up into the stands. Unlike the players, everyone else was bundled up in fall coats, scarves, and hats. Tim spotted his mom and Kayla and waved.

Roger was in the stands, too. His chess friends had come to the game with him again, all in their ridiculous bee hats. This time it made Tim smile. Roger had also brought a couple of friends from their diabetes group.

Tim recognized Ricky and Lola and waved to them.

Tim turned his attention back to the game. Henry was leading the offense down the field. With a beautiful pass, he sent the ball to Joe, the team's best wide receiver. Joe caught it and sailed into the end zone for a touchdown. A cheer went up on the sideline. The kicker scored the extra point and the crowd cheered again. The score was now 31–24, with thirty seconds left on the clock. Tim put his helmet back on and headed out onto the field. He had to stop the other team from scoring.

The center hiked the ball to the quarterback. Tim heard the clashing of plastic helmets and padding as the lines dove into each other.

The wide receiver raced off the line. Tim raced to keep up, but the wide receiver stayed open. The quarterback spotted him, and Tim saw him arc the ball into the air just before being tackled. It was now or never. Tim didn't know his legs could carry him as fast as they were now moving. He raced to cover his man, all the while watching as the ball sailed toward them . . .

Swoosh. Tim caught the ball in his arms just before he was tackled by the wide receiver. He had intercepted the ball! As he got to his feet, he heard a roar of cheers erupt from the stands.

With just seconds left in the game, Tim had solidified the win for the Hornets. As he came off the field, his teammates tackled him with hugs and chest-bumps.

"Nice job, man!" Henry said, slapping Tim on the back as he headed out to the field once more.

"Bring it home!" said Tim.

And bring it home they did. The Hornets held on to the ball for the final seconds of the game, preventing the Briarwood Bears from scoring again. The whistle blew, and the Hornets raced onto the field to congratulate one another.

Tim looked up into the stands to see Roger and his friends going nuts. He was proud to have so many people cheering for him. It was a stark contrast to just a few weeks ago, when he had been embarrassed to see Roger and his friends cheering him on in their bee hats.

Tim looked for his mom and sister. They had raced down to the field, where they cheered and screamed, waiting for the chance to congratulate him.

Just then, Hank ran up to Tim and tackled him. "We did it!" said Hank.

"You know it!" said Tim. Now he only had one more thing to accomplish—to pull off the party and show his two groups of friends that they were *all* cool!

Chapter 18

When Tim walked into his house after the game, he couldn't believe how great the living room looked. Kayla and her friends had decorated it with streamers and balloons. Tim's mom had filled a table with all kinds of snacks.

"Wow, it looks awesome in here," Tim said. Kayla had invited a few of her friends, too, and they looked extremely excited and nervous to be hanging out with eighth graders. It was pretty adorable, Tim had to admit to himself.

Before long, Tim's friends began to show up. When Roger arrived, he slapped Tim on the back. "Nice game tonight, Tim-bo!" he said. "You were awesome."

"Thanks, Roger," Tim said. "Hey, Lola! Hey, Ricky!" he added, greeting his friends, who had come to the party with Roger.

"Great job out there," said Ricky. "It's really too bad our teams don't play each other. You guys would be tough opponents!"

Tim smiled. "Thanks for coming tonight! It means a lot to have you guys here."

"Our pleasure," said Lola. "I can never say no to a good party!"

Tim looked around. While he had been chatting with Roger, Ricky, and Lola, his house had begun to fill up. His football friends and Roger's chess buddies were milling about, talking and laughing. As he looked around, he was surprised to see Sam approaching him. He was holding a plate of veggies in his hands.

"Hey," Sam said, nodding to Tim. Then he looked at Roger. "Roger, how's it going? Thanks for coming out and supporting the team tonight. You guys sure have team spirit."

"Thanks!" Roger said, as friendly as can be. "Sam, this is Ricky, and this is Lola. They're friends from outside of school."

"Hi," Sam said.

Tim smiled at Sam, nodding at him in thanks for being kind. He was glad Sam was making an effort.

Suddenly, Tim saw Jenny walk through the front door. Before his brain could get all muddled and stop him, he walked over to her.

"You came!" Tim said.

Jenny smiled. "Of course," she said. "I

invited some of my cheerleading friends, too. I hope that's okay." Jenny gestured behind her, where a few giggling girls were walking up the path to the front door.

"Sure thing," he said. "The more the merrier. I—I'm really glad you came."

Jenny blushed. Tim was pretty sure his cheeks were red, too.

"Me too," she said. "Great job tonight, by the way. You totally won the game for us."

"Thanks," Tim said. "It's pretty much been the best day of the school year so far, and it's only getting better."

Jenny and her friends went off to get something to drink, and Tim glanced over to where he'd left Sam talking to his friends. Henry and Hank had joined them, and everyone was laughing at something Roger was saying that involved crazy hand gestures and lots of loud, squawking noises. Tim was thrilled to see his friends getting along so well.

As the night wore on, Tim talked with Roger's chess friends. Even though he'd been to one of their matches, he didn't know them very well yet. But he was glad to get to know them better. After all, if Roger could get to know his friends, he could get to know Roger's, too! They reminded him of a shyer version of Roger—funny, quirky, and kind. Tim had never had so many friends before.

It was hard to believe that, a few months ago, Tim would never have pictured Roger among his group of friends. But he was glad to be able to include Roger in that group. Tim didn't love having diabetes, but it had sure brought one good thing with it: Roger. Tim's prediction that eighth grade would be different from any other school year appeared to be coming true. And it was better than he could have imagined.

Questions to Think About

1. How does Tim feel the night before his first day back at school? What is he worried about? How did going back to school after your diagnosis make you feel? Did you have any concerns?

2. Tim promises himself that he won't make a big deal about his diabetes to his friends. How does keeping things to himself make him feel? When you first

went back to school, did you talk to your friends about your diabetes? Do you talk about your feelings now?

3. After Tim is diagnosed with type 1 diabetes, his family decides that they could all eat healthier. Did you change much about the way you ate? Did learning to balance your meals affect what the rest of your family was eating?

4. Tim wishes that he had someone to talk to who has been through what he's going through. Did you ever feel that way? Do you have any friends who have diabetes?

5. Tim spends the morning of his first day back at school nervous about his blood sugar. How did you handle your first day back? Did you have any concerns?

6. Tim worries that his friends will judge him for hanging out with Roger. Have you ever been friends with someone who your other friends didn't like? How did you handle it?

7. Tim notes that bringing his lunch to school makes him feel different from his friends. Has the way you manage your diabetes ever made you feel different from your friends? How did you handle that feeling?

8. Roger says that when he was first diagnosed with diabetes, he felt lost and alone. How did you feel when you were diagnosed? Have your feelings changed over time?

9. How does Tim feel about having to sit out part of his first game because his blood sugar is low? Have you experienced a low during a game or practice? How did it make you feel?

10. At Roger's urging, Tim agrees to attend a diabetes group. Have you ever been to a support group? Do you have other friends with diabetes who you can talk to?

11. Tim realizes that maybe his friends don't ask about his diabetes because they think he doesn't want to talk about it. Do your friends ask you questions about your diabetes? Are they interested in learning more about it?

12. Tim says that his diabetes brought him at least one good thing: Roger. Has your diabetes had a positive impact on any part of your life?

Lilly is an expert in type 1 diabetes, and no one knows families like Disney. Now, these two companies have come together to create special resources for families like yours.

From Disney Publishing Worldwide comes a series of books for children of different ages and at varying stages of type 1 diabetes. There's also a section for parents of children with type 1 diabetes on Disney's popular website, family. com. Visitors to www.family.com/type1 can find articles, videos, and tips from caregivers raising children with type 1 diabetes. This unique site highlights ways families can establish new routines and let kids be kids. Together, Lilly's expertise in type 1 diabetes and Disney's magic can help keep your child and your family feeling inspired and empowered to live a full, active life with type 1 diabetes!

Ask your doctor about getting your hands on the other books in the series and visit http://www.family.com/type1 today!

Also available:

Power Forward

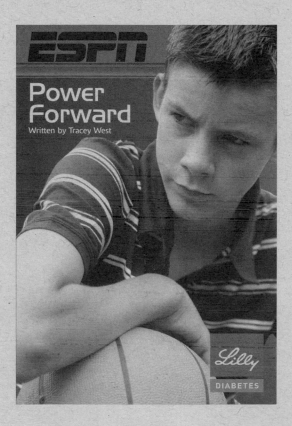

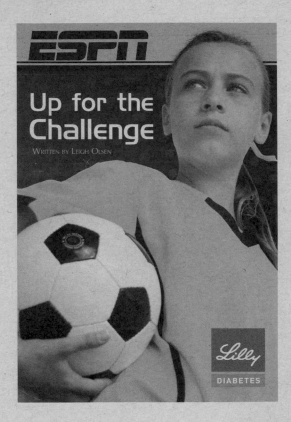

Uptight (Oliver's All Right)

Coco and Goofy's Goofy Day

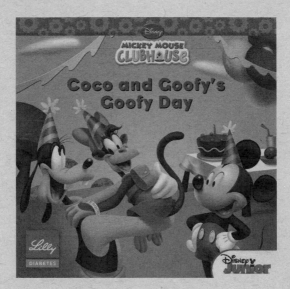